# Disney
# Winnie the Pooh

# Something Is Missing!

Adapted by Lisa Ann Marsoli
Illustrated by Mario Cortes, Valeria Turati
and the Disney Storybook Artists

PaRragon

Bath · New York · Singapore · Hong Kong · Cologne · Delhi
Melbourne · Amsterdam · Johannesburg · Auckland · Shenzhen

There once was a boy named Christopher Robin who had a room full of wonderful toys to play with. Of all of these, the stuffed animals were his favourites – especially a bear called Winnie the Pooh.

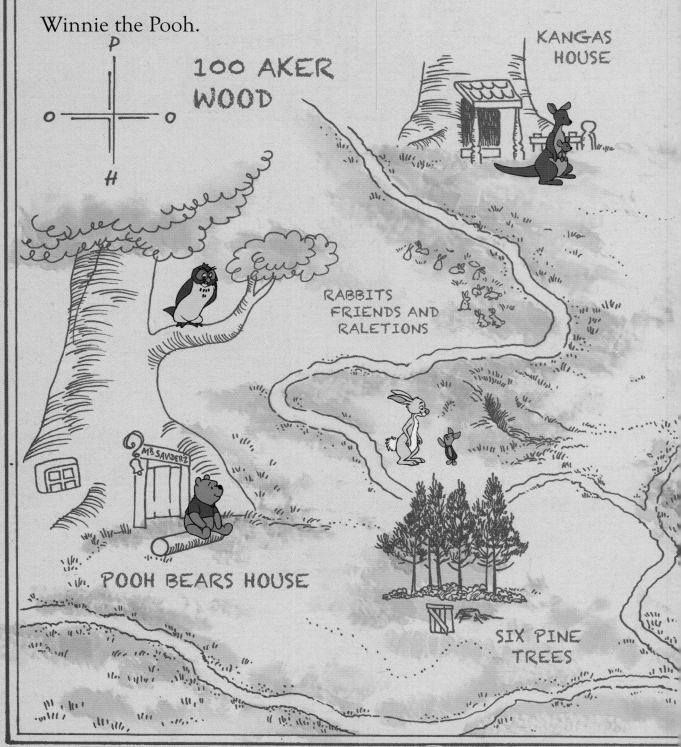

KANGAS
HOUSE

100 AKER
WOOD

P

O—|—O

H

RABBITS
FRIENDS AND
RALETIONS

MB SAVDERZ

POOH BEARS HOUSE

SIX PINE
TREES

The boy, Pooh and the rest of their well-worn friends
spent many happy hours sharing make-believe adventures
in a beautiful place called the Hundred-Acre Wood.

Early one morning, Pooh slept in his cosy house inside a tree, dreaming of honey. Honey was his favourite thing to think and dream about, as well as his favourite thing to eat. And on those rare occasions when Pooh forgot about honey, his rumbly tummy was quick to remind him.

Finally, it was time for breakfast. Pooh checked his cupboard first, sure there would be a pot full of the sweet stuff.

"Empty," observed Pooh. "Well, luckily, I keep some extra in the house."

Finally, he came upon a jar he felt sure was full.

He tipped it back farther... and farther... and farther...

until the weight of the pot *tipped* him right over!

Sensing that Pooh had been distracted from his task, his stomach issued forth several more hungry and impatient sounds.

Pooh realized that drastic measures were in order. Since there was no honey to be found inside, he had no choice but to venture out into the Hundred-Acre Wood to find some more.

Suddenly, Pooh spotted some bees. Since where there were bees, there was usually honey, Pooh felt hopeful – and a little cautious. He had learned from experience that beehives could be very unfriendly places when the bees were home!

Pooh reached inside the beehive.

Buzzzzzzzzzzzzz

But the bees were not fooled – most likely

because tree branches don't reach into beehives!

A big, angry swarm poured out of the hive, and Pooh took off running. He knew he couldn't out-run the bees, so he would have to out-think them – which was no small task for a bear-of-very-little-brain.

Buzzzzzz

Luckily he stumbled upon the perfect hiding spot.

He vowed that just as soon as the bees were gone, he

would pay his friends a visit. Surely one of them would

have some honey to spare.

Pooh soon came upon a friend.

"Eeyore," said Pooh, "what has happened to your tail?"

"What *has* happened to it?" Eeyore wondered.

"Well, it isn't there," Pooh explained.

Pooh knew what he had to do. "I, Winnie the Pooh, will find your tail," he promised. "And then we shall get some honey."

Just then, a familiar voice drifted down to them from a nearby tree. "Oh, hello, Pooh, Eeyore," Owl said. "I'm penning my personal memoirs."

"Perhaps you could take a short break from your important work and help us find Eeyore's tail?" asked Pooh. "You have such a talent for speaking and telling us what to do."

Owl handed Pooh a pad and pencil. "Write this down carefully," he instructed. "Now the customary procedure in such cases is as follows..."

"What does '*crustimoney proceedcake*' mean?" Pooh asked.

Owl explained it meant "the thing to do" and continued.

"The thing to do is, we write a notice promising a large something to anyone who finds a replacement tail for Eeyore. Is that clear?"

"Oh, that sounds like a wonderful plan, Owl," said Pooh, imagining a tasty honey reward as he listened.

Owl flew off to Christopher Robin's house to ask for his help.
The boy immediately set to work making several large signs that
read A VERY IMPORTANT THING TO DO. Each one had a spelling
mistake or two, but since no one in the Hundred-Acre Wood was
any better at spelling – it was certain that no one would notice.

Pooh helpfully took
the signs and began posting
them all around the
Hundred-Acre Wood.

Pooh finished posting the signs and turned to leave, bumping directly into B'loon. Just as Pooh was inviting him along for the Very Important Thing To Do, Tigger leaped out of a bush. Tigger thought B'loon was going to bounce the stuffing out of Pooh!

"Don't be afraid, Tigger," said Pooh. "It's only B'loon."

Tigger assured Pooh that he was only pretending to be afraid.... "So's my opponent would *underestimamate* me, and then I'd get the drop on him! I must go... because the Hundred-Acre Wood needs a hero... and I'm the only one!" And with that, Tigger bounced off into the Wood.

Christopher Robin waited for all his friends to arrive, then called the meeting about the Very Important Thing To Do to order. He gestured to Eeyore, who turned to display his barren backside. "We will have a contest to find a new tail for Eeyore," Christopher Robin said.

Owl interrupted to remind Christopher Robin that contests usually involved some kind of prize for the winner.

Everyone had a different idea as to what a desirable prize might be.

Pooh gave Christopher Robin the piece of paper with his drawing. The boy smiled.

"Why, Pooh, that's a grand idea!" he exclaimed. "The prize for a new tail shall be a pot of honey!"

# Winnie the Pooh

# Tails, Tricks, and Traps

Suddenly, Pooh had an idea. "I have just the thing!"he exclaimed. He dashed towards home, where the most perfect tail he could think of was hanging on his wall.

"Thanks, Pooh," said Eeyore after Pooh had outfitted him with a clock. The friends declared Pooh the contest winner.

Then they presented hungry Pooh with his reward – a nice, full pot of delicious honey!

But before Pooh could scoop out even one pawful of the gooey stuff – CRUNCH! – Eeyore had sat on his clock tail and crushed it.

CRUNCH!

"Oh, dear," Owl said. And with that, he snatched the honeypot back from a very disappointed (and still very hungry) Pooh.

"We could give B'loon a try," suggested Piglet.

But Eeyore discovered the problem with having a balloon
for a tail is that you have to go where it wants to go – and not
the other way around!

The friends tried a great many more things for Eeyore's tail:

a yo-yo,

an umbrella,

a weather vane,

a party hat,

a moose head,

and an accordion

...until at last they ran out of them. "It's okay," said Eeyore. "I'll learn to live without it."

Kanga then gave her scarf to Eeyore to use as a tail.

Later, Pooh noticed a piece of yarn lying on the ground.

He picked it up and followed it... straight to Eeyore.

But Eeyore was unaware that he was dragging something along with him.

Pooh tried to warn him, but he was

knocked

right

off his

feet!

When Pooh landed, he found himself quite close to
Christopher Robin's house. "Christopher Robin will have
some honey!" he declared.

Christopher Robin was not there, but he had left a note
on the doorstep. Pooh was puzzled. He decided to take the
note to Owl's house.

Pooh arrived just in time to see Owl being presented with the prize for finding Eeyore's latest tail.

"Let me see," said Owl. "There's never been a note written that I could not decipher." He placed the honey on the mantle and invited Pooh to help himself.

"It says," began Owl, "'Gone out, busy Backson. Signed, Christopher Robin.' Our dear friend Christopher Robin has been captured by a creature called the Backson!"

The friends gasped in fear.

"It's malicious," Owl added, "ferocious, and worst of all... terribly busy! I saw a picture of one just the other day."

Owl described a thoughtless creature that scribbled in library books, spoiled milk, stopped clocks and put holes in socks! But Rabbit came up with a clever plan. They would collect things that the Backson liked and leave a trail of them to lure it into a pit. Then the Backson would be trapped – and they could get Christopher Robin back!

The friends found the perfect spot and got to work. Piglet dug a very deep pit, covered it with a cloth, then weighed down the corners with four large rocks. He took a honeypot and explained that they were going to use it to help disguise the trap even more.

"Well, it certainly fooled me and my tummy," said Pooh.

The pair quickly caught up with the others, who were already leaving a trail of objects – socks, dishes, toys and clocks, among many other things – across the Hundred-Acre Wood. Everyone worked together, knowing the sooner the trail was complete, the sooner the Backson would be captured – and the sooner Christopher Robin would be safe!

"Hurry along, everyone!" called Rabbit. "Don't dawdle."

Tigger, meanwhile, had decided to track the Backson on his own. He was pretty sure he had found him too, when he pounced on something moving in the Wood. Unfortunately, it turned out to be Eeyore, who had accidentally been left behind by the others.

"You and me are gonna catch that Backson together!" Tigger declared.

"Do I have a choice?" asked Eeyore.

Tigger bounced off, thinking Eeyore was right behind him. But a few bounces later, Tigger discovered he was all alone.

Tigger returned to his friend. "Buddy," he said, "if you're gonna pounce, you gotta have some bounce. We just need to get you *tiggerized*!"

Tigger started with the easy part; giving Eeyore stripes. "Looking great," said Tigger. "Now you gotta learn to bounce like a tigger." He attached a large spring to Eeyore and set him in motion.

The donkey went

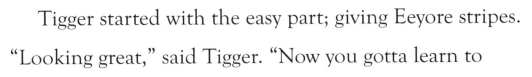

up and down...

up and down...

up and down...

and, shortly thereafter, just up.

Back on the ground, Eeyore continued to bounce out of control. Eventually, the friends ended up in Rabbit's garden. Tigger dressed up as the Backson and coached Eeyore on how a tigger would "bounce" the monster into surrendering. The poor donkey ricocheted from fence to scarecrow to washing line to Tigger to the woods beyond.

Meanwhile, Pooh had been distracted by his rumbling tummy, and enlisted Piglet's help in fetching some sweet honey. But Piglet became lodged deep inside a bee hive!

Luckily, a few swipes of Pooh's stick brought the hive down.

The pair ran into a very annoyed Rabbit.

"What are you two doing?" Rabbit demanded as he pulled the hive off Piglet. "Beehives are not on my list of Backson-friendly items." He tucked the beehive up into a tree and gave Pooh and Piglet a friendly shove. "Move along! Move along! We've so much to do!"

Over by Rabbit's house, Tigger searched for his new partner, Tigger II – also known as Eeyore.

Tigger didn't find Eeyore, but he did find Eeyore's spring "tail". "You're going to need this if you're going to get the Backson. Unless the Backson got you first!"

# Winnie the Pooh

# Lost and Found

Rabbit was very pleased. His plan to catch the Backson and rescue Christopher Robin was almost complete! He and his friends had left a trail of items leading to the trap they had set for the Backson. Now all they had to do was wait for it to show up.

"Rabbit, can we stop for lunch?" Pooh asked.

"We cannot rest until Christopher Robin is found," insisted Rabbit. "Try thinking of him instead of honey."

"Very well," Pooh agreed. He did his best to concentrate.

Then something very strange happened. Pooh's shadow started looking like a honeypot!

Then, every time Pooh's friends spoke, all he could hear was, "Honey, honey, honey." Next, everything beneath Pooh's feet melted into a giant wave of honey! He swam and dived and floated in the honey. He gobbled and gulped and guzzled the honey. Pooh was so blissfully happy that he sang a honey song and danced a honey dance. Life was sweet!

Pooh's beautiful daydream soon faded and he went on his way.
After a few steps, he came upon a large honeypot centred on a cloth.
Pooh was so excited at the prospect of honey that he didn't recognize
the very Backson trap he and Piglet had set earlier that day!

Meanwhile, Pooh's friends had arrived back at the pit and were looking everywhere for him. Then, all at once, they heard a loud *THUD!* The friends clung to each other in fear.

"The plan worked!" Rabbit exclaimed. "We caught the Backson!"

"You went back for the honey, didn't you?" asked Piglet.

"I told you it was empty."

Just then, Eeyore arrived at the pit and showed off his newest tail to the group. Rabbit thought Eeyore's tail might be the answer to Pooh's predicament, so he threw the anchor into the pit.

But it was so heavy, it yanked the friends down into the hole. Only Piglet, who had been tossed high into the air, remained outside the trap.

Now it was up to Piglet to save his friends. Just then, Roo
remembered that Christopher Robin owned a jump rope.

Rabbit urged Piglet to go to the boy's house and get it. Owl
flew out of the pit to encourage the terrified Piglet. When he was
done, he flew back in. It was now clear that Owl did not need
rescuing from the pit – but no-one seemed to notice.

Piglet trudged nervously into the foggy woods, knowing he had a very important thing to do. As he looked all around, the very small animal backed into a very large tree root. Startled, he turned and saw what looked like a red-eyed monster glaring down from up in the tree! But it was only his friend B'loon.

Loyal little Piglet realized that no matter how
frightened he was, he had to go back and save
his friend.

Piglet slowly inched his way over to B'loon.

A few tugs later, as Piglet pulled B'loon from
the tree, an enormous shadow fell over them.

Piglet turned and faced the monster. "B-B-B-BACKSON!" he shouted. He held on tight to B'loon and raced away as fast as he could.

But there *was* no Backson – only Tigger dressed in a Backson disguise.

But now Tigger thought the Backson was right behind *him*!
He ran after his friend so that they could flee together.
"Piglet!" he cried.

"He knows my name!" shrieked Piglet. "HELP!"

B'loon lifted Piglet up and away, but it was a very bumpy
ride. Then Piglet spotted the pit in the distance. He thought
if he could just reach it – and his friends – he would be safe.
He had nearly made it when Tigger crashed into him.

Down into the pit they both tumbled.

When the dust settled, everyone was relieved to see
that the "Backson" chasing Piglet was really only Tigger.
And Tigger was relieved to see all of his friends.

Owl was not the least bit upset by the setback. He began to tell a very long story, unaware that his friends were growing bored.

Pooh idly looked up and saw Tigger's discarded honeypot sitting at the edge of the pit. So he decided to build himself a ladder out of the letters that had fallen into the pit with them.

Suddenly, Rabbit saw Pooh's ladder of letters. "We can get out!" he cried.

The friends were relieved to be out of the pit – until they heard a rustling in the bushes.

"Backson!" they cried.

But it was only Christopher Robin, led by B'loon.

"How did you escape the Backson?" asked Rabbit.

"What on earth is a Backson?" Christopher Robin asked.

"The most wretched creature that you could meet," Owl said solemnly.

"What gave you the idea I was taken by a Backson?" replied Christopher Robin.

Pooh handed him the note. Christopher Robin giggled as he explained that he had written that he would be "back soon" – not "Backson." It had all been a misunderstanding!

Before the friends headed home, Rabbit declared, "We owe a very special someone a token of our appreciation. Someone who got us out of this pit and helped us to find Christopher Robin. So, I bestow this pot of honey upon our dear friend... B'loon."

Pooh and his tummy were dumbstruck.

Pooh's hungry tummy soon

led him away, looking this way and that for the honey it so desperately

wanted. Pooh kept on searching until he ended up at Owl's house.

It took all of Pooh's remaining energy to climb up the tree to Owl's

front door, where he pulled the new bell rope. There was something

very familiar about it.

As Owl invited Pooh in for some honey, the bear realized Owl's new bell rope was Eeyore's tail!

"Of course," said Owl realizing his mistake. "I was just keeping it safe for him."

As much as Pooh hated to leave the honey, he had to return Eeyore's tail to him right away.

Pooh took the tail straight to Christopher Robin, who securely attached it to Eeyore with a hammer and nail.

"What do you think?" Christopher Robin asked.

Eeyore considered his old tail, with which he was newly reunited. "Seems about the right length. Pink bow's a nice touch. Swishes real good, too," he said.

That was good enough for Christopher Robin. "Bring out the grand prize!" he instructed.

"Thank you all ever so much," said Pooh. He climbed straight into the pot. He swam and dived and floated in the honey. He gobbled and gulped and guzzled the honey. All his honey dreams had finally come true!

Later, Christopher Robin told Pooh how proud he was that Pooh had put his friend before his tummy.

"Thank you," Pooh replied. "I don't think I shall be hungry again for a good long while."

Just then, Pooh's stomach rumbled.

"Silly old bear!" said Christopher Robin.